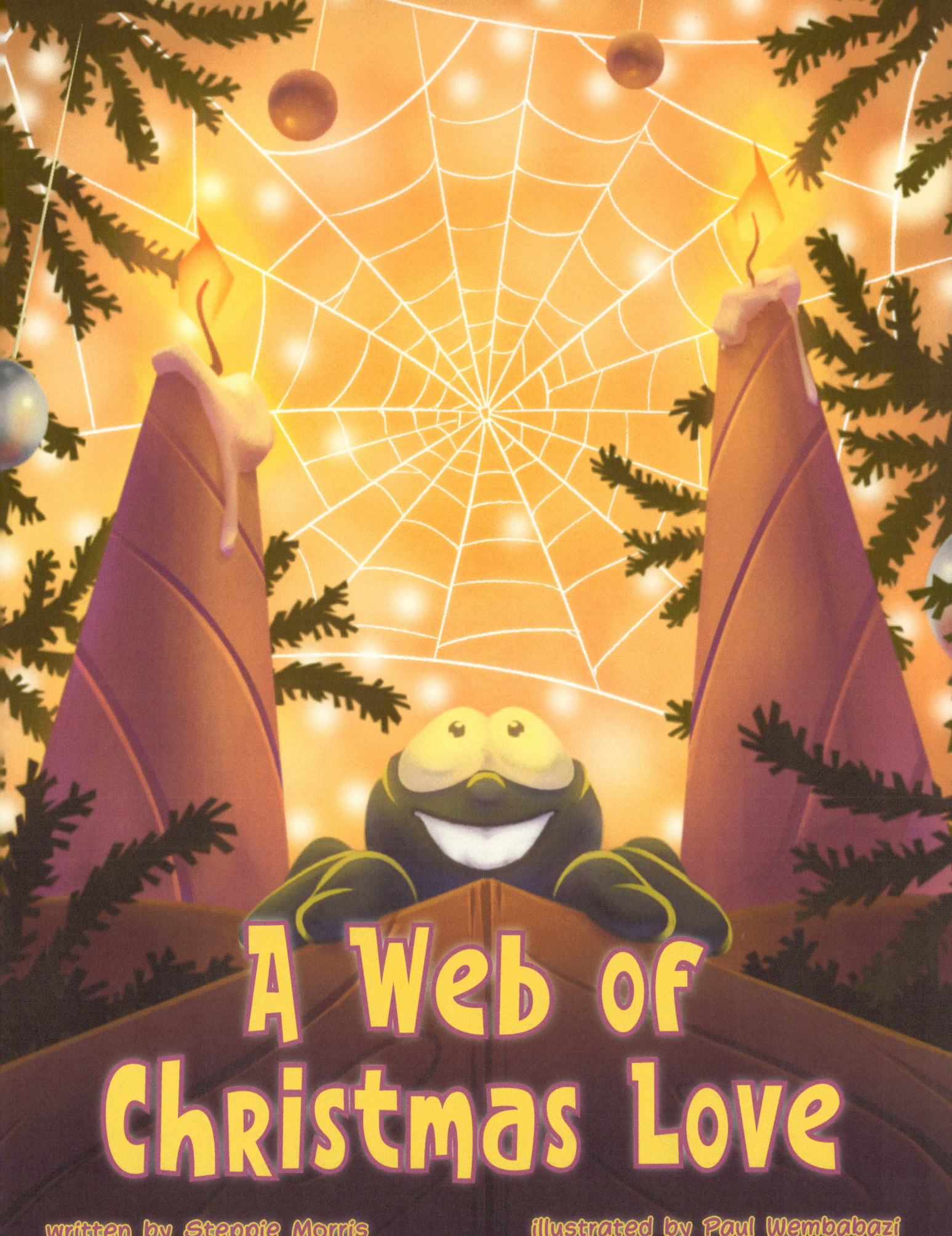

This edition first published in 2024
by Lawley Publishing,
a division of Lawley Enterprises LLC.

Text copyright © 2024 by Steppie Morris
Illustration copyright © by 2024 Paul Wembabazi
All Rights Reserved

Hardcover ISBN 978-1-958302-01-9
Library of Congress Control Number: 2023931972

Lawley Publishing
70 S. Val Vista Dr. #A3 #188
Gilbert, AZ 85296

LawleyPublishing.com

For all imperfect creatures, and with gratitude for the grace, mercy, and love of Jesus Christ.—SM

A spider cowered in a corner,
watching from afar.
The activity below him,
he thought, was quite bizarre.

She set to work, both high and low, she washed and scrubbed all day, dusted shelves and mopped the floor, swept his cobwebs clean away.

Spider watched from rafter nook—
the safe place to where he'd fled.
The bustle and commotion
did fill his small form with dread.

The pine boughs and the trimmings and the fire burning low,

the tall tree in the corner with ornaments hung just so!

He saved the best for last because
there was so much to see.
He savored every moment
as he climbed throughout the tree.

But as his joyous rounds were done,
a light filled up the room.
Had someone seen his spindly form?
That's what he did assume.

A gentle hand reached out to him,
a welcoming reminder
of safety and assurance—
no other soul was kinder.

This hand he knew, he knew it well,
no hand more strong or true.
It lifted him up in the air
to share the Master's view.

His tiny heart dropped to the floor
to see what had become
of the marvelous and merry room,
to see what he had done.

The lovely tree, once colorful, a beautiful delight,
now veiled in threads of cobwebs,
made a gray and gloomy sight.

His head hung down.
He had not known.
He never had intended
to ruin all her efforts,
to mar all she had mended.
To his dismay, the Master stretched
to touch a fragile web.
And suddenly, the dreary tree
was draped in silver instead!

The lovely sight from earlier could not even compare to the dazzling, striking spectacle that now shimmered there!

He stared at the gleaming room.
His mind began to wonder.
Why would God give miracles
when he'd made such a blunder?

A thought crept in that made him feel
an inch and one foot tall.
The love of God flows freely
to all creatures—large and small.

The Lord of Lords and King of Kings
once in a manger lay
as babe before He grew into
the Truth, the Light, the Way.

Ever gently, the small spider
was placed back on the tree
near a shiny ball of glass.
His reflection could he see.

His breath he caught.
He gazed in shock.
Could this be just a jest?
He studied each and every leg,
then checked out all the rest.

A golden shimmer covered him
from head to all eight feet.
His tiny heart filled with thanks
for an undue gift so sweet.

The light did fade.
The room grew dim.
Again, he was alone.
He marveled at the special night,
of what he had been shown.

Spider's mem'ry turned away
from embarrassment and fears
to messages of truth and hope,
not fading with the years.

His gift was far more precious
than treasure dripping from the trees.
The Lord sometimes works miracles
to show you what he sees.

No sin, mistake, or weakness
is beyond God's loyal reach.
He sees us with a willing heart,
with patience does He teach.
Whether you are old or young,
rich or poor, live near or far,
God forgives our mistakes,
and He loves YOU for who you are!

THINGS TO THINK ABOUT

1. What is the difference between an accident and doing something on purpose?

2. Did the spider in this story do something on accident or on purpose?

3. How does Jesus feel about the creatures around us?

4. How did Jesus show this little spider how He felt about him?

5. How does Jesus feel about you?

6. Do you know how special you are?

7. How does Jesus show you that He loves you?

Stephanie first heard the legend of the curious spider when making a little golden spider ornament for her tree. Each holiday season, that little spider, is moved around the tree by her children. It reminds her that Christ loves every single one of us and that all are welcome in this magical season of celebration.

Stephanie was given her nickname, Steppie, by her brother, who also had a way of making everyone feel special and included. She enjoys the beautiful winters in Arizona with her husband, five children, and two grandkids, where she helps her husband remodel their home, goes on an occasional desert hike, and gets her family together with the lure of delicious food and a movie or game night. She loves the intoxicating smell of wassail, pulling her collection of children's Christmas books out, and gets excited the moment the first Christmas decoration goes up.

Steppie Morris is the author of *I Hope Your Dreams Are Sweet*, *The Children in the Box*, and *Come Dance in the Rain*.

Paul Wembabazi is a full-time husband and a proud father from Uganda. He holds a bachelor's degree in Industrial and Fine Arts, majoring in Illustration, advertising design, and anatomy. As a child, he loved cartoons, and when he learned that they didn't magically appear on screen but were drawn by a group of artists, his dream grew to become an artist, creating colorful cartoon characters and worlds. He is also a fine arts teacher and a bass guitarist with the Milege Heritage Foundation/Milege Afro Jazz band.

Printed in the USA
CPSIA information can be obtained
at www.ICGtesting.com
CBHW041258201024
16140CB00012B/37